A VERY FURRY CHRISTMAS

Holiday Cat Tales

John D. Ottini

Copyright

A Very Furry Christmas © 2015 John D. Ottini
Cover Art by Lou Harper Copyright 2015

All Rights Reserved
No part of this book may be used or reproduced in any manner whatsoever without written permission, except in the case of brief quotations embodied in critical articles and reviews.

This book is a work of fiction. While reference might be made to actual historical events or existing locations, the names, characters, places and incidents are either the product of the author's imagination or are used fictitiously, and any resemblance to actual persons, living or dead, business establishments, events, or locales is entirely coincidental.

ISBN-13 978-1517712785
ISBN-10 1517712785

Dedication

These stories are dedicated to my cat Bella who has brought love, joy, and laughter into my life.

To animal lovers around the world who love their pets and can't imagine living their lives without them.

CONTENTS

A VERY FURRY CHRISTMAS

SLIPPER'S LAST BREATH 7

THE UNWRAPPED GIFT 15

A CHARCOAL CHRISTMAS 37

CHRISTMAS MOURNING 53

A MESSAGE FROM THE AUTHOR 63

ABOUT THE AUTHOR 65

BOOKS BY JOHN D. OTTINI 67

Slipper's Last Breath

Previously published in Holiday Tales Anthology 2014 Fireside Publications

It's the day before Christmas, a time of happiness and joy, but in my heart I know this Christmas will not be a joyful occasion.

The fireplace crackles and pops as my eyes are drawn to the front window, where large and fluffy snowflakes fall, covering the trees and yard. Tears build in my eyes, but I dare not allow them to escape, in fear that they will not stop once they begin flowing. In need of distraction, I switch the radio on, and the joyous sound of Christmas music fills the room. For a few moments my spirit is lifted and my thoughts drift to happier times.

I take a sip of hot coffee and half-heartedly continue placing ornaments on the tree. Decorating the Christmas tree has never been one of my strong points, but I promised my wife, Mary, that every Christmas I would decorate the tree in her honor, until the day we met again.

It's been five long years since she's been gone and yet I still see her face, smell the scent of her hair, and crave her gentle touch. I've lived 64 years without serious illness, but in the last few years, I've battled through my share of pain and heartache. When Mary was diagnosed with pancreatic cancer, I couldn't catch my breath for three days. As the months went by, and the treatment became worse than the illness, I knew that her pain and mine would never go away.

Slipper's Last Breath

When she passed away, my world was shattered. My wife, best friend, lover, and soul mate was gone, and so was my reason for living. Retired, alone and depressed, each day was a struggle to survive. There were days when I couldn't find a single reason to get out of bed. I know that Mary would be upset to see me this way, but nothing made me happy.

Mary and I never had children, but fortunately our friends and family did the best they could to keep me busy moving forward, and in time I began to heal. Now when I think back on that difficult time, I realize that no one was more instrumental in keeping me sane and alive than our cat, Slipper.

Slipper was twelve when Mary died, and that poor tabby wandered around the house for days, searching for her best friend, wondering where she had gone. At the time, I could not imagine what she was going through, grieving over the loss of her companion, because I was far too busy drowning in my own sorrow to pay attention to her needs. I fed Slipper and cleaned her litter, but other than that, I was totally numb to her existence.

As you may have surmised, Slipper was Mary's baby; I was just the guy who competed for Mary's attention and on occasion accidently stepped on her tail. We got along okay, but we were never close, and we certainly weren't best buddies.

After her death, it took a good six months for Slipper to feel comfortable occupying the same room as me. At nine months she allowed me to pet her and would sometimes curl up in my lap on cold winter evenings. On rare occasions when I left the house, she would be waiting for me at the front window and would greet me with meows and leg rubs at the door. At night she would sleep at the foot of the bed and wake me each morning by walking on my chest and licking my nose. At first the routine annoyed me, but eventually I found comfort in the attention she gave me every morning. On the odd occurrence when she didn't wake me up in this manner, I worried that something might be wrong, but it was usually nothing, and I would find her staring out the window at some rabbit or squirrel.

At the one year mark, we were indeed the best of friends.

Now, I cannot imagine my day without her brushing against my leg, jumping on the newspaper, or playing hide-and-seek. She is a very vocal companion and has no trouble letting me know when she wants my attention or when it's mealtime. I've always considered myself a tough guy, but I know without a doubt that I love my cat and that she is the focal point of my life.

I stare across the room and the smile evaporates from my face. She lies quietly on her favorite pillow in front of the fire place, staring back at me, her eyes following my every move. At seventeen years of age, her vision is failing; her coat is no longer shiny or well-groomed, and her energy level is almost nonexistent. It takes something very special to get the old girl off her pillow and prancing across the room. When she does move, it's always in a slow and cautious manner, her way of hiding the pain of her illness.

Recent visits to the veterinarian's office did not bring us good news. The vet informed me that she had developed feline leukemia and that her days on this earth were numbered. At her age, there was not much he could do medically, so he suggested that I do my best to keep her as comfortable and happy as possible.

I know that the inevitable is coming, but Slipper is my last connection to Mary, and I'm finding it very difficult to say goodbye.

I walk over to the fireplace and sit down beside her. She looks up at me with her sad, brown eyes and purrs softly as I pet her. Her body feels cold, and her once beautiful coat is no longer soft and glossy.

"Hello, baby. How are you feeling today?"

She just stares back at me.

"Girl, I would do anything to make you feel better, I hope you know that." I whisper as my throat goes dry, "I have no idea what I will do without you, my friend."

She looks at me as if to say, *it's okay, Dad. I'm still here, don't be sad, I'll be fine if you'll be fine . . . I'm not afraid.*

Moisture fills my eyes and a lump develops in my throat. I know that I have to let her go, but it's more difficult than I ever imagined.

"I'm right here, girl. Don't be afraid. I don't want you to suffer any more," I tell her as I gently touch her nose. Her nose is dry and rough, but it is still the cutest little nose I have ever seen.

"Don't worry about me, I'll be okay," I say, lying to the best of my ability.

Are you sure Dad? Do you promise you'll be okay? I can't leave knowing you won't be okay without me.

Be strong, I keep telling myself. Let her know that it's alright to say goodbye. I smile bravely, stroke the soft spot above her nose, and nod my head in approval. She takes one last look at me and lays her head on my lap, then closes her eyes and takes her last breath.

My body begins to tremble and the tears roll down my cheeks. I hug and kiss Slipper on the forehead and cover her in her favorite blanket. I grab my coat and step out into the cold air, but there is no escaping the unbearable ache inside my heart. My body slides down the wall and I cry uncontrollably. Why did this have to happen on Christmas Eve?

I don't remember how long I've been crying, but I feel the cold numbness in my hands, and I know I have to get to a warmer place. I can't bear going back into the house, so I run to my car and slip behind the wheel. A feeling of absolute loneliness consumes me; it's as if Mary has died all over again. If I have to go through this one more time, I don't think I will survive.

I jam the keys in the ignition, start the engine and back out of the driveway. I have to speak to someone, and I know who that someone is. I crank up the heater and pull out onto State Road 10, then drive 12 miles south to Mission Valley Road, where I turn right onto Old Cemetery Road. The old car has finally warmed up, but I am so consumed with the thought of telling Mary that Slipper is gone, I hardly notice that my hands are no longer cold.

The cemetery sidewalk is buried in snow, but I manage to shuffle through until I reach my Mary's gravesite. I brush the afternoon snow from the tombstone to reveal Mary's photograph and her epitaph etched in stone.

MARY BELSON MASTERSON

1950 - 2009

BELOVED WIFE OF WILLIAM MASTERSON

A precious one from us has gone.

A voice we loved is stilled.

A place is vacant in our hearts, which never can be filled.

Until we meet again.

After all these years, I still get choked up every time I visit her grave. Today I fall to my knees, look to the sky, and feel the icy snowflakes land on my face.

"Hello sweetheart, it's me, Bill. I came here to let you know that your baby, Slipper, passed away today and is coming home to see you."

Slipper's Last Breath

A cold wind blows through the cemetery, followed by what sounds like a painful scream. Momentarily shocked, I glance around, but I see no one. I am alone. I place a hand over my mouth when I realize that the sound had involuntarily escaped from my throat in my moment of grief.

"She passed away quietly at home on her favorite pillow. I don't think she suffered much, but I miss her already."

Warm tears flow down my cheeks. I raise my collar up to keep the chill from my neck, but nothing brings me warmth or comfort at this moment of despair. I feel lost and distraught; everyone I love in this world is gone.

"My love, I promised you I would continue on without you that I would try to be happy until we meet again, but I don't think I have the strength to go on like this. How do I know you are even listening to me? How can I be sure that I will ever see you and Slipper again? I'm alone Mary, so alone in this world."

Mary hated when I questioned my faith. She never understood why I couldn't just believe and be happy. I had always wished I had that kind of strength and belief in the concept of everlasting life, but I didn't. One day, I remember asking her why she believed so strongly in the afterlife, since there is no way to prove its existence.

Her reply shocked me, "Because the alternative is too sad and frightening to imagine."

"My love, I miss you so much and I love you with all my heart. Please send me a sign, any sign, which will help me to believe that my life is still worth living!"

I hear a car door slam behind me and the sound of children's voices echo through the cemetery. Upset and shaken, I get up off my knees, brush the snow off my pants, blow a kiss to Mary, and head to the car. In the automobile, I begin having serious thoughts about committing suicide. There is no point in living in a constant state of misery!

It is 5:30 p.m. and dusk has turned to night. I switch on the headlights and start home. I decide at that moment that I will have Slipper's body cremated right after the holidays and will scatter her ashes over Mary's grave. It will be the closest thing to a reunion they will ever have, and I know that it will please Mary. Once that is done, I will deal with myself.

A short time later I pull into the driveway, switch off the engine and sit in silence. I hear the ticking and clicking noises as the engine cools down. I wonder if I can go back into that house without having a complete mental breakdown. I sit awhile longer, trying to motivate myself to go inside, but in the end it's the thought of freezing to death in the car that sends me heading toward the front door.

As I reach the door, I can hear Josh Groban singing *Oh Holy Night*, and my heart sinks. I don't want to be alone on Christmas Eve, especially not this Christmas Eve. My fingers are stiff from the cold, and I drop my keys while trying to unlock the door. I reach down to pick them up and hear a soft, scratching sound coming from inside the front door.

"What the heck is that?" I say out loud. I listen and hear it again. I open the door slowly, not knowing what to expect, and there at the door stands Slipper staring at me. I stand frozen, unable to move, a look of disbelief on my face, and then she lets out a deep and loud meow. I'm not sure what it means, but I'm guessing she said, "Come in and close the damn door, it's cold outside". I pick her up and hug her, as my heart explodes with love. I laugh and I'm dancing around the room, like an idiot, then I begin crying, but this time they are tears of pure joy.

"How can this be?" I say out loud. "I don't understand how this is possible?"

Slipper's Last Breath

Slipper licks my face and looks at me as if to say, *Dad, don't ask how or why, just be as happy as I am, that we have each other one last time for Christmas.*

"You're right, girl." I say as I kiss her on the nose and tell her I love her. "You're so right."

Then it hits me, this is my sign? My one last gift from Mary and Slipper? My true Christmas miracle?

I pour myself a cup of coffee, and Slipper a small saucer of milk. Then we sit quietly enjoying each other's company and listening as the holiday music brings forth another Christmas morning. It is one of the happiest moments of my life.

Two days go by and our beloved Slipper passes away in her sleep, and as promised, I am at the cemetery scattering her ashes over Mary's grave.

As I drive away, I realize that Slipper has once again saved my life. I don't know for certain what brought her back to me when I needed her most, but I know that I am no longer sad and depressed. I now believe that my loved ones are together forever, and that one day soon, I too will see them again.

After all, the alternative is indeed too sad and frightening to imagine.

The Unwrapped Gift

It's two weeks before Christmas and the weather has taken a turn for the worse. There's not much snow on the ground, but it's brutally cold outside with temperatures dipping into the negative double digits after the sun sets.

Spice, my five-year-old Labrador retriever, waits patiently by the front door with her leash in her mouth, knowing that it's time for us to make the long walk to the mailbox. I've been working late hours at my store and the last thing I want to do is go back out into the cold, but I know that poor Spice has been cooped up all day and needs to go outside to do her business. Reluctantly, I put my coat on, secure the leash to Spice's collar, and head into the cold night air.

David and I built this house three years after we got married. It's an old farm-style home that sits on two acres of land, eight miles outside of town. We'd chosen this lot because there's plenty of space for me to cultivate my vegetable and spice garden, and for David to build his art studio, but most importantly for our future family to laugh, grow, and play together. It was everything we'd both dreamed of, or so I thought.

During our walk to the mailbox, Spice stops several times to relieve herself and to smell interesting things along the way. We named her Spice because the first day we brought her home, she ran straight into the garden and buried her nose in the parsley, basil, and rosemary plants.

The Unwrapped Gift

We finally arrive at the entrance to the driveway, and Spice begins her ritual of barking at the passing cars whose headlights illuminate the mailbox. I reach inside the box, retrieve the mail, then tuck it under my arm and begin the long walk back to the house. Our pace is a little brisker on the way back because the cold wind has shifted directions, and now snow is blowing directly into our faces.

Back inside, I switch on the gas fireplace and watch as Spice lies down in front of the warm glow. I walk to the kitchen, start the coffee maker, pull a frozen dinner out of the freezer and pop it into the microwave. It's not what I'd normally eat, but I'm too tired to fuss with cooking tonight.

As the microwave does its thing, I sit down at the kitchen table and sift through the mail. There are two Christmas catalogs, three greeting cards, and an energy bill addressed to me. The rest of the mail appears to be junk mail for David, so I toss it into the waste basket.

I can't believe that after all these months, I'm still receiving mail for my ex-husband. Every time I receive a piece of his mail, I'm reminded of our failed marriage.

For awhile I'd put his mail aside. Once a week I'd bundle it up and drop it off at his mother's house. Looking back now, I have no idea what I was thinking when I did that. Perhaps I was hoping that he'd have a change of heart and run back to me, asking for forgiveness. That dream ended the day he served me with divorce papers. That's when reality set in.

I shake my head in disgust at the thought that I offered to take the bastard back if he would attend marriage counseling. After everything he'd done, I was willing to forgive him because I still loved him and believed that marriage is forever. His refusal to accept my offer was an all-time low in my life. My self-esteem was shattered. I should have been furious with him, but instead I was ashamed of myself and wondered what I'd done to make him stop

The Unwrapped Gift

loving me. I take a sip of coffee and my thoughts wander back to that unbelievable day when I caught him cheating on me.

I was struggling with a miserable cold, and I knew I should have stayed home that day, but I stubbornly went to work anyway. My symptoms got worse as the hours dragged on, so I decided to leave my assistants in charge and take the rest of the day off.

I should have known something was wrong when I saw my girlfriend's car parked in front of my house. I had no idea why she'd be there during the day, but I felt too miserable to even try to make sense of it. I'll never forget the look on their faces when I entered the house.

There in our living room was David standing with his pants around his ankles, my girlfriend Cheryl bare-breasted and kneeling before him. They quickly scrambled to cover their naked bodies, and David had the audacity to imply that this was not what it appeared to be.

I don't remember what happened next, but I do recall throwing up, the splatter hitting David, and slapping Cheryl across the face. The rest of the day is a bit sketchy, but I was told that I passed out and was taken to the ER where they treated me for a high fever and dehydration. I remember the hospital keeping me overnight for observation and releasing me the next morning.

You can imagine how upset I was when David and Cheryl showed up and insisted on driving me home. I was too tired, confused, and upset to argue, so I let them have their way.

No one spoke on the drive home, which was just as well, since I'm quite certain that in my state of mind, I would have knocked the shit out of David had he opened his mouth.

Back at the house, they sat me down like a five-year-old, and Cheryl began to explain how sorry they were that I found out the way I did.

The Unwrapped Gift

"This was not the way we wanted you to find out," she said.

"Why? Is there a good way to find out that your friend has been screwing your husband?"

"That's not what I meant."

"How long has this been going on?" I asked, fuming.

"Three and a half months," replied Cheryl, as David stood quietly at her side.

"Three and a half months?" I screamed, staring directly at David. "How much longer were you planning to wait before telling me?"

"Look, it's nobody's fault," said Cheryl. "It just happened and we can't take it back. No one wanted to hurt you, Beth. David fought off telling you for this long because he knew you'd be devastated. Isn't that true, Davy?"

David said nothing.

Did she just call my husband Davy? Lucky I didn't have a gun in the house, or they'd both be dead.

"This is all for the best, Beth," continued Cheryl. "Davy doesn't love you anymore, and if this hadn't happened with me, it would have happened with someone else. Sooner or later, anyway."

"So you did me a favor," I said sarcastically.

"I wouldn't put it that way, but. . ."

"Shut your big fat ugly mouth, Cheryl! I can't believe I was ever your friend. How could you do this to me? Never mind, I don't give a shit what you have to say about this. I want to hear it from my dear, sweet husband. Go ahead, Day-Vee. Go ahead and tell me that what she says is true? Here's your chance to tell me that you don't love me anymore."

I'm not sure what I expected him to say, but when he opened his mouth, nothing came out. He simply nodded his head up and down and looked at me as if to say, I'm sorry.

In that moment I was crushed. I wanted to cry, but I didn't want to give them the satisfaction of seeing me defeated.

My pain and sorrow manifested itself in a scream, "You damn coward. Get out of my house. Get the hell out of my house."

"Now, Beth, calm down," said Cheryl.

I screamed even louder, "Get out now! Right now. Before I do something you'll both regret."

The sound of my screaming voice upset Spice, and she began to growl and bare her fangs.

She started towards them but I stopped her, grabbed her by the collar and said, "Come here, girl." I threatened to turn her loose, if they didn't leave.

They held up their hands and backed away slowly. I'll never forget the pathetic look on David's face as they drove away. He looked back at me as if shocked by my actions. How did he think this was going to end? Did he think we'd hug, wish each other well, and part the best of friends?

I feel tears well up in my eyes and scold myself for being silly enough to still let this upset me. After all those weeks of counseling I shouldn't still feel this way.

I think of all the wasted plans we'd made, how I'd worked so hard to build my business in order to support him while he struggled to get his artistic career off the ground. We'd both agreed to put our dreams of having a family on hold until we had established ourselves and paid off a good chunk of the loan on our

The Unwrapped Gift

house and land. Yes, it was all very upsetting, but looking back now, thank goodness we never had children.

I wipe the tears from my eyes just as the timer on the microwave dings, distracting me from my dark moment.

"Saved by the bell," I say, as I pour myself another cup of coffee, grab my dinner and take it to the table.

Awhile later, I'm sitting in the living room watching TV as Spice sleeps peacefully by the tree stand. It's almost Christmas and I've yet to put up a single decoration. The only thing I've managed to do is retrieve the tree stand from storage and place it at the front window. I guess I was hoping that seeing the stand everyday would motivate me to do some decorating, but so far it hasn't done anything but depress me. After everything that's happened this year, I don't feel much like celebrating.

I should just put the stand back into storage, I thought. Guess it can wait until morning.

Spice knows it's time for bed when she hears me switch off the TV and walk up the creaking staircase. I know that in a few minutes she will follow me upstairs.

The next morning I wake up to a fresh coat of snow in the yard. It's Sunday, my only day off, so I convince myself that I'm going to make it a good day. I brew a fresh pot of coffee, switch on the radio, and sit down to enjoy some cornflakes and Christmas music.

Spice is draped over her bowls, munching on food and lapping up water. When she's done, I watch her walk to the front window and lay down next to the tree stand. She keeps smelling and staring at the stand, probably wondering when that 'tree thing' is going to arrive. In previous years, David and I had made it a tradition to drive out to Miller's farm and cut down our own Christmas tree. I get the feeling that Spice notices something is missing this year.

The Unwrapped Gift

"No tree this year, girl," I say sadly.

It's times like this that I feel that she misses David the most. He was always at home during the day, and she must wonder what happened to that guy who used to hang around here all the time. It was difficult at first, and it took awhile before she stopped looking for him every day, but eventually she must have realized that he's no longer here. Lately, I've sensed that she once again feels the loss, and I wonder if it has something to do with it being Christmas.

Christmas was a big deal at our house. We always decorated and lit up the house and yard. We made it a point to take Spice with us to pick out our Christmas tree, and to see Santa and the lighting of the big Christmas tree in the town square.

This year was different. No decorations, no tree farm, no caroling, and no town square. There was no Christmas joy in our house, and poor Spice sensed it.

"You're doing a great job of making me feel guilty, girl."

Spice barks once, then lays her head back on the floor. I look at her and think she looks and feels as miserable as I do. Maybe it's time we do something about it. "Maybe getting that Christmas tree isn't such a bad idea," I say to her.

At hearing the words, Spice lifts her head and looks at me as if to say, *a Christmas tree would be awesome, Mom. Can we get one? Ha, can we?* Her tail begins wagging back and forth as she jumps up and runs around the room. I haven't seen her happy in months, and I realize when she's happy, I'm happy.

"Okay, girl, let's go get us a tree."

Miller's tree farm is a twenty mile trip and requires a good half-hour truck ride to get there. Twenty miles of pure heaven for Spice, who gets to sit in the front seat and ride with her face near the open window. If it were up to Spice, her whole head would be

The Unwrapped Gift

sticking out the window, but it's too cold for me to allow her to do that. I don't want her getting sick.

When we arrive at the tree lot she begins barking impatiently and jumping up and down on the seat. When I open her door, she runs straight at Jim Miller, the proprietor.

Jim gets down on one knee, gives Spice a big hug, and rubs her behind the ears.

"Hey, girl, don't you look beautiful," he says with a smile on his face.

I'd heard Jim's wife had lost her battle with cancer earlier in the year, but this was the first time I'd gotten the chance to see him.

"Hello, Jim. Sorry to hear about Lilly. She was a sweet, wonderful person who'll be missed by everyone who knew her.

"Thanks, Beth. I still can't believe she's gone. This Christmas is going to be a tough one for me."

I place my hand on his shoulder. "I can't say that I know exactly how you feel, but I can only imagine how painful your loss must be."

"That's kind of you, Beth. How are you doing?" he asks. "I heard about you and David."

"It was difficult at first, but it's getting a little easier with each passing day. All I can do is keep moving forward."

"What else can we do but keep on living," he says with a look of understanding on his face. "I have to say, as far as I'm concerned, David was a fool to leave you. He obviously had no idea how good he had it."

I'm a little surprised by his comment, but also happy to hear it.

The Unwrapped Gift

"Thanks, Jim. I guess this is going to be one of those Christmas's to forget, for both of us."

"Yup," he says with a feeble smile. "I'm thinking it would be best for us to change the subject before we both start bawling."

"Sounds like a great idea to me," I reply. "Spice and I are here looking for a Christmas tree. Do you think you can help us with that?"

"I believe you came to the right place," he says chuckling. "Would you like me to assist you in picking out a tree?"

I look around and notice there are a lot of people shopping for trees.

"Are you sure you can spare the time? It looks like you've got your hands full around here."

"My associates are more than capable of assisting our customers while I accompany you and Spice on a tree hunt. Just give me a minute to fetch my chainsaw, and we'll see if we can't find you a nice one."

"Thanks. We'd really appreciate your help."

Jim returns with his saw and says, "Think I have a tree in mind for you, but it's a bit of a walk."

"Great. Spice and I love to walk. Don't we, girl?" Spice replies with a bark.

As we walk towards the west end of the farm, Jim keeps Spice occupied with chasing and retrieving a stick he's brought along. We pass the time talking about business, the weather, and town politics, but inevitably the conversation returns to our mutual losses.

"Are you still at the house?" he asks.

The Unwrapped Gift

"Yes. David left everything to me, except the artwork in his studio. I guess he really wanted a fresh start. No baggage from the past."

"That's good, I guess," says Jim, nodding. "I wish I could put some of my memories behind me."

"As much as Lilly loved you, I'm sure she would want you to live and be happy, Jim. That doesn't mean forgetting what you had together, but rather just moving forward and trying to find some peace and contentment."

"That's so much easier said than done."

"I know. I'm still working on it, too, but something as simple as being out here with you and Spice feels like a step forward."

"I know you're right, but I'm not sure I'm ready yet."

"I hate to pull out that old cliché, but you'll have to take it one step at a time. I don't think there's any time limit on grieving."

We walk a bit further in silence before Jim says; "There she is," pointing at a beautiful seven-foot scotch pine in the distance.

"Oh my God, it's gorgeous."

"I told you she's a beauty!"

Spice barks in approval.

"Let's cut this baby down and get back before the weather turns nasty. I see clouds coming in from the north and that usually means snow on the horizon."

We get the tree back to the retail trailer, where Jim trims, bundles, and secures the tree to the bed of my truck. I thank him and ask him how much I owe.

"It's on the house," he says.

The Unwrapped Gift

"Oh, no way! I can't accept it for free. That tree's probably worth a hundred dollars."

"Then it's a hundred dollars well spent."

"Are you sure about this?"

"I couldn't be more sure," he says, smiling. "The short time I've spent talking to you and playing with Spice has done me a world of good. Thank you for listening. It's a lost art, you know."

"Do you mean listening?"

"That and taking the time to care about what you're hearing," he replies.

"You're a good guy, Jim. God bless you."

"Thanks, Beth. I hope you and Spice have a very Merry Christmas."

"Merry Christmas, Jim" I say while giving him a hug.

Jim turns and begins to pick up the tree scraps he'd trimmed off my tree.

"Wait! The least I can do is help you clean up this mess."

"Not necessary, Beth. You and Spice should be on your way before the snow hits. I don't want you getting caught in the storm."

"Nonsense! We're not afraid of a little snow, are we, Spice? I insist on helping you, and there's nothing you can say to change my mind."

"Nothing like a stubborn woman," he says, chuckling. "Suit yourself."

As I pick up some of the pieces and toss them into the nearby dumpster, I hear a faint, meowing sound coming from

The Unwrapped Gift

inside the dumpster. I stop what I'm doing and stand quietly to listen, but all I hear is the sound of a truck engine. The sanitation truck has arrived to empty the dumpster. I hear the beeping as the truck rolls slowly towards the dumpster, so I step away from it.

Again I hear a meow, but this time it's louder and more frantic.

I jump between the truck and the dumpster and shout, "Stop."

The driver slams on the brakes and jumps out of his cab.

"Hey, lady, are you trying to get yourself killed?"

"What's going on?" asks Jim.

"I think there's a cat in the dumpster," I reply

"As far as I know, there isn't a cat around here for miles. Are you sure you heard one?"

"Yes and no," I reply.

The driver is clearly upset with me interrupting his schedule and says, "What the heck does that mean?"

Spice begins barking and clawing at the dumpster.

"I thought I heard a cat's meow coming from inside the dumpster, but I'm not sure."

"Maybe we should have a look," says Jim. "Better safe than sorry."

Jim asks the driver to shut off the engine, and he says, "Fine. You got five minutes. Knock yourselves out."

Jim and I climb up onto the metal bin and begin calling, "Here, kitty, here, kitty" then listen, but hear nothing. After the third attempt we jump down and apologize to the driver who gets back into his truck, starts the engine, and continues towards the dumpster.

I call Spice away from the dumpster, but she refuses to move. She continues barking louder and more frequently, and then jumps frantically against the side of the bin.

The driver honks his horn, but Spice refuses to budge.

"Something's not right, Jim. I've never seen Spice act this way."

Jim tells the driver to stop the truck and once again we jump onto the dumpster. This time we both hear a soft meow. Jim jumps in, and a moment later climbs back out with a small cardboard box in his hands.

Inside the box is a tiny white kitten, which I'm guessing couldn't be more than six weeks old. I pick up the kitten, hold it against my chest, and it begins to purr and rub against my face.

"It's a girl," I say. "The poor thing is cold, frightened, and hungry. I wonder how she got in there."

"Probably someone dumped her here and left her to die, maybe some asshole whose daughter didn't want the kitty any more," replies Jim.

I'm momentarily shocked at Jim's tone of voice. I've never heard him say anything in anger before.

He continues by saying, "I don't understand how people can do something so cruel and still sleep at night. If you ask me, that's absolutely criminal."

He's right, I thought, this poor thing hadn't done anything to deserve this fate.

Jim turns to Spice and kisses her on top of the head.

The Unwrapped Gift

"You saved her life, girl. In my world that makes you a hero. Come with me. I got a special treat for you."

Spice follows him to the trailer and returns with a large bone in her mouth.

"Jim, I think you've made a friend for life."

The driver snarls at me and says, "Well, ain't this cute. Can I pick up the damn garbage now?"

I want to give him the finger, but the idiot isn't worth it. Instead I carry the kitten to the truck and start the engine so I can heat up the cab. I call Spice, and she comes running and jumps into the front seat with the bone securely between her teeth.

Before leaving I roll down my window and call Jim over. I ask him what he's doing Christmas Eve.

"I'll be right here working up until we close, at around four o'clock."

"After you close up, how about coming over to my house for dinner?"

"That's mighty kind of you Beth, but you don't need to do that."

"You're right. I don't, but I want to. Will you please come?"

A big smile crosses his face and he says, "I'd love to."

I return the smile and say, "You've made Spice and I very happy. We'll see you then."

Jim waves goodbye and says, "I'll be there. In the meantime make sure you take good care of Sugar."

"Sugar. Who's Sugar?" I ask.

The Unwrapped Gift

"The little white bundle of joy you've got sitting in the box beside you. I think you should name her Sugar."

That's the perfect name for this kitten, I thought. Sugar and Spice... I love it.

The following day, I take the morning off so Spice and I can take Sugar to the vet. Dr. Westfield runs some tests and informs me that Sugar is in excellent health.

"Lucky you found her when you did. The poor thing probably wouldn't have survived a cold night in that dumpster."

"If it wasn't for Spice causing such a commotion, she probably would've been crushed in the back of the garbage truck. Isn't that right, girl?"

Dr. Westfield pats Spice on the head and says, "You're a good dog, aren't you?" Spice responds by licking his face in appreciation.

"Sorry about that, Doctor," I say.

"No need to apologize. I get that all the time from my four-legged friends."

"You must love your job."

"Best job in the world," he replies.

After leaving the vet, we stop by Pet Smart to pick up cat litter, a litter box, cat food, and a couple of cute feeding bowls. I also pick up a special hero's treat for Spice.

Both girls are asleep in the truck by the time we arrive back home. Although they'd gotten along well the previous night, I didn't feel comfortable leaving them together unsupervised. Spice is not pleased with my decision to lock Sugar in the spare bedroom. She whines and seems genuinely sad that she can't be with her new friend. I tell her to be good and guard Sugar until

The Unwrapped Gift

Mommy gets home tonight. Then I give her a special treat to help her forget about Sugar for awhile.

When I arrive home that evening, Spice is not at her usual spot at the front window. Instead I find her sleeping against the bedroom door. I let Sugar out of the bedroom and all hell breaks loose, but in a good way. Spice runs around the living room all excited, and little Sugar tries her best to keep up. It's such a blessing to see how playful and happy they are together.

After dinner I decorate the tree and make sure that the expensive breakable ornaments are placed up high so neither Sugar nor Spice are tempted to play with them. Once the decorating is complete, both girls plop themselves down under the tree and take a nap. They look sweet together as Sugar lies sleeping tucked under Spice's big old chin.

It's been a long and tiring day, so I leave the girls asleep under the tree and head upstairs to bed. A few minutes later, as I lay in bed saying my prayers, I hear Spice jump up on the bed. Then I hear Sugar meowing and clawing. When I look down over the side I see her trying to claw her way up, but the climb is too high. I pick her up, lay her on my chest, and listen to her purring and kneading until she falls asleep. Spice is already snoring softly by the time I feel myself slipping into dreamland.

I smile and think, thank you Lord for the blessings you've given me.

* * *

Two weeks fly by and before I know it, it's Christmas Eve. Jim calls to tell me that he's closing up and on his way. Since our visit to the tree farm, Jim has called me several times to inquire about Sugar, but I suspect, or at least hope, that the calls are about more than Sugar.

The Unwrapped Gift

I'm not sure how he feels about me, but I know that I'm beginning to have feelings for him. Feelings that I haven't felt in years, and didn't think I would ever feel again.

Slow down, Beth, I think, it's only been two weeks and Jim isn't ready for a relationship yet. Don't pressure him or you might push him away.

Jim arrives promptly at six o'clock, carrying two boxes. One contains a homemade apple pie and the other has a big red bow tied around it. He hands me the box with the pie and places the other under the tree.

Embarrassed by the unexpected gift, I say, "Jim, I wish you'd told me you were bringing gifts. I didn't get you anything."

"Don't fuss. It's just a little something I made to thank you for inviting me to dinner."

Before I can reply, he turns into the living room and says, "How are my girls doing tonight?"

Then he gets down on his hands and knees and begins playing with Sugar and Spice, who are delighted by the attention. I'm glad he's too preoccupied to turn around, because if he did, he would have noticed me standing there with a big, loving grin on my face.

Dinner is ready at seven o'clock and we sit down to eat. Jim asks if I'd mind him saying the blessing. I tell him that would be very nice.

"Thank you, Lord, for good friends and this wonderful meal before us. Thank you for giving us the strength to survive the bad times and to enjoy the good," he says, looking straight at me, "and bless our furry companions for all the love and joy they bring into our lives. Lastly, bless my Lilly and tell her I miss her every day."

"Amen," I reply, touching his hand. "That was really wonderful. I'm sure that your message will be delivered."

"Amen," he says, squeezing my hand, "Now let's eat before this wonderful food gets cold."

And eat we do.

We eat turkey with stuffing and cranberry sauce. Mash potatoes with gravy, green bean casserole, and sweet rolls with butter. When we're done, we have just enough room left for coffee and Jim's incredible apple pie.

"This is absolutely delicious. Where did you learn to bake like this?"

"It's an old family recipe handed down from generation to generation. After mother had me, instead of a girl, she found out she couldn't bear any more children, so she told me it would be my job to carry on the Miller pie-baking tradition. She's the one who taught me how to bake these incredible pies."

I raise my eyebrows in surprise and say, "Pies? You mean you bake more than one kind?"

"You should taste my blueberry pie. It's to die for."

We spend the next half hour washing the dishes and cleaning up the kitchen, then move into the living room for more coffee and conversation. We both agree not to discuss the sad times, so we talk about our childhoods, our large families, and our favorite Christmas moments when we were kids. I'm pleasantly surprised at how much we have in common and how we share many of the same values.

Poor Sugar and Spice are fast asleep under the tree by the time eleven o'clock rolls around.

Jim looks at his watch and says, "I guess I better get going."

The Unwrapped Gift

I want so badly to ask him to stay, but I know it's the wrong thing to do. I don't want to do or say anything that might damage our friendship or the possibility of a future relationship. I tell him that I had a wonderful evening.

"Thank you for inviting me, Beth. I really enjoy talking to you."

"Me too, Jim." I hesitate. "We should do this again soon."

"Sure," he replies in a non-committal fashion. "That would be nice."

"Let me walk you to your truck," I say, grabbing my coat.

"No need to do that. It's cold out there. I wouldn't want you to get sick on Christmas Day."

I really didn't want him to leave, so I buy myself more time by saying, "Hey, would you mind if I open the gift you brought me?"

He looks at his watch, then smiles and says, "I guess it's close enough to Christmas Day. I sure hope you like it."

I slowly untie the red bow and open the box. Inside is a beautiful handmade wreath decorated with bows and miniature ornaments. Hanging from the top of the wreath is a wooden plaque with the words, MERRY CHRITSMAS TO BETH, SUGAR & SPICE - CHRISTMAS 2015, burned into the wood. Tied to the plaque is a small book containing the poem, *Twas The Night Before Christmas*, by Clement Clarke Moore.

"This is so sweet, Jim. Did you make this yourself?"

"Yes. I made the wreath from some of the branches I trimmed off your Christmas tree. The wood burning skills I learned as a Boy Scout finally came in handy," he says laughing.

"Well, I think it's beautiful. Thank you so much."

The Unwrapped Gift

This is the part where I want to reach up and kiss him, but I fight off the temptation, and instead I tell him to be careful driving home.

"Thanks for everything," he says, then surprises me by kissing me gently on the cheek and giving me a big hug.

If I could freeze this moment in time, I would do so.

He opens the door, turns and says, "Goodbye girls," staring back at Sugar and Spice. "Take good care of your mom. Goodnight, Beth."

"Wait," I say.

Jim catches the emotion in my voice and says, "I really like you Beth, but this is all I can offer you for now."

"I know and I understand," I reply, disappointed. "Will I see you soon?" I ask and hold my breath.

"Absolutely," he smiles.

"What are you doing tomorrow night?"

"Tomorrow?" he replies pausing for a moment, "I guess I'll be at home tomorrow."

"Oh." I say lowering my head, "At home."

"Yes, at home, but I'm pretty sure that I might be available in the evening."

I smile and say, "Six o'clock?"

"I'll bring my blueberry pie. You're going to love it, Beth," he says as he walks out the door.

I close the door behind him and whisper, "I already do."

The Unwrapped Gift

Its eleven thirty, but I'm too excited to sleep, so I change into my pajamas, make some hot cocoa, and sit on the sofa wrapped in a warm blanket. The girls join me on the sofa, and we sit watching the lights flicker on our beautiful Christmas tree.

I look down at the girls and say, "It's almost Christmas, and I think it's time we start our own family tradition."

I reach into the pocket of my pajama bottoms, pull out the little book that Jim had attached to our wreath, and I begin to read.

"Twas the night before Christmas and all through the house, not a creature was stirring not even a mouse."

I stop to look down at my angels and smile. Spice has her eyes closed, and Sugar is stretching and yawning. I put the book down and stare out of the window at the falling snow.

I close my eyes, and I'm suddenly overcome with emotion as warm tears of joy run down my face.

For the first time in a long while, I'm at peace with myself and I see a future blessed with possibilities.

I whisper, *"Happy Christmas to all, and to all a goodnight."*

A Charcoal Christmas

She was born under the loading dock behind Johnson's Market. Her mother was a black and white tabby named Mattie who'd run away from an abusive owner several years ago and settled behind the store. The store owner, Mr. Johnson, was an old curmudgeon who by all appearances hated cats, but every night after closing his store, a bowl of food and water mysteriously appeared on the dock for the little cat family

She and her siblings were mothered well, right up until the sad day when Mattie was run down by one of the delivery trucks. When Mr. Johnson discovered what had happened, he immediately grabbed a shovel, scooped up Mattie's remains and placed them in a burlap sack. That evening after the store closed, he said a prayer and buried her in the empty field behind his dumpster.

The litter suspected that something was wrong when their mother didn't come home for dinner. Fortunately the six kittens were five weeks old and capable of feeding themselves, thanks to Mr. Johnson's generosity.

She was the runt of the litter. The only one whose fur was a solid smoky grey color. Her brothers and sisters were mixtures of black, white and grey and resembled their mother. She must have inherited her father's characteristics, even though she had no idea who he was.

A Charcoal Christmas

Mr. Johnson continued to feed the cats, and by the seventh week he'd given each of them a name. He named her Charcoal. It wasn't a very flattering name, but there wasn't much she could do about it and besides, it was better than having no name at all.

The everyday life of a feral cat is a fairly routine one. Charcoal's days were spent hunting, playing, eating and sleeping. She was enjoying her life hanging out with her siblings until one day she broke the first rule of the unwritten feral cat code: Never trust a stranger bearing treats.

Lured by the scent of tasty treats, Charcoal was abducted, placed in a cardboard box and taken away from her home and family. Frightened and alone, she meowed and whined as the stranger who abducted her took her on a bumpy car ride. The ride didn't last very long and when he opened the container, she found herself in a strange environment and refused to leave the box.

"Come out, little girl," said the stranger. "I won't hurt you."

Charcoal listened to his calm voice, but didn't budge from the box.

"Are you hungry?" he asked, placing a bowl of food near her.

She didn't want to fall for that trick again, but the food smelled really good and she hadn't eaten since last night.

"Come on," he said as he gently picked her up and placed her near the food.

She couldn't resist the temptation and began to eat. As she ate, she kept an eye on the man, ready to bolt if he made any sudden moves. Then the man did something to Charcoal that no one had ever done before. He ran his hand slowly down her back while she ate. At first it made her nervous, but as he continued it made her feel really good. Before she knew it she was purring.

As he continued to stroke her, he said, "Tina is going to be so surprised when she sees you. You're going to make a wonderful birthday gift."

She had no idea what the man was saying, but if he continued to treat her in this way, she'd be more than happy to stay here.

"Don't worry. My girlfriend will take good care of you."

When she'd finished eating, he picked her up and placed her inside a different container. This one was bigger than the other one and was surrounded by iron bars. It had a tray with sand in it, a bowl of water and a blanket. Being kept in a confined space was not something Charcoal was accustomed to. She began to meow and salivate, and take fast, nervous breaths.

The man switched off the light and left her alone to deal with her panic attack.

The quiet and the darkness seemed to calm her nerves. She circled the container three times before realizing there was no way to escape. Knowing she was trapped, she closed her eyes and tried to rest.

The next morning the man opened the container door and gave her more food. He stroked her while she ate, then picked her up and put her in a completely different container. This one was a cat carrier with mesh windows and soft sides.

He picked her up in the carrier and brought her to his car. Charcoal didn't like this container because it moved back and forth while he carried her.

"Time to see Dr. Sara," said the man. "Dr. Sara is my sister and a veterinarian. She'll take good care of you." Charcoal had no idea what a Veterinarian is, but she was about to find out.

A Charcoal Christmas

She didn't enjoy riding in the car the first time and this time was even worse. She meowed and whined all the way to their new destination. Charcoal was so upset that her bladder let loose in the container. She was afraid that the man would be mad when he saw what she'd done, but instead he said, "Poor girl. I'm sorry you got so scared. Dr. Sara is not going to hurt you. She just wants to make sure you're okay."

Dr. Sara pulled Charcoal slowly out of the carrier and did that stroking thing to make her relax. It worked wonderfully right up until she began poking, prodding and sticking things into Charcoal's body. She didn't like that and began to struggle and bite. She felt something sharp pinch her on the back, and before she knew it she was fast asleep.

When Charcoal woke up, she was back in the man's house. She wasn't sure what had happened, but knew that someone had done something to her belly because it was sore. She kept trying to lick it. Someone had put something around her neck that kept her from reaching her stitches. She wasn't happy about it, but was too weak and drowsy to do anything about it. For the next few hours she kept falling asleep and waking up. Every time she woke up the man was right next to her, stroking her and rubbing the top of her head.

She had no idea how long this went on. All she knew was that she was in a warm, safe place with plenty of food and someone who treated her well.

Over the next few days she would spend her mornings and afternoons locked in the container while the man was away from home, but at night he would let her explore around the house and sit on the window sill. Charcoal was beginning to think that maybe this wasn't so bad. It was nice having someone take care of her.

Then one night the man bathed and brushed her and tied a pink ribbon around her neck. He picked her up and placed her inside the same container he'd used to take her to that place where they poked and prodded her, and took her to his car.

He put her in the front seat and said, "It's party time, little girl."

She meowed and whined, but he ignored her. Before she realized what was happening she was being carried inside a strange house and hidden in a dark closet. This was the first time since she'd been abducted from Johnson's Market that she was really terrified. She sat quietly listening to the loud voices, music, and strange noises, wondering what was going to happen to her.

Later that evening things got quieter outside the closet and the man came to get her. He took her into a big room, put the container on the floor, opened it and picked her up.

Then the man said, "Happy Birthday, sweetheart," and handed Charcoal to a person sitting on the sofa.

Charcoal could tell by the way the woman held her that she was not very comfortable with cats.

"Oh, how cute," she said as she sneezed.

"Are you okay, Tina?" asked the man.

"I'm fine," she replied, "I think I may be coming down with a cold."

"Well that's a relief. For a second there I thought maybe you were allergic to cats."

"Don't be silly, I absolutely adore her," she replied, dropping Charcoal down on the sofa and sneezing again.

"Come with me," she said, taking the man by the hand.

They went into another room and closed the door. Charcoal sniffed around the sofa and listened to the strange sounds coming from the room where they had disappeared. She wondered what was happening, but stayed away from the door.

When they finally came out of the room they were both very friendly towards her.

"Will you take me out on the boat tomorrow?" Tina asked.

"After that," the man said smiling, "I'll do anything you want, sweetheart."

"Are you picking me up in your Jag?"

"Absolutely." He replied.

The man kissed Charcoal on the head and said, "Take good care of Tina. I'll see you two tomorrow."

Then he got up and left without her.

Charcoal tried running towards him as he headed for the door, but Tina grabbed her and said, "You stay here with me," and began rubbing her fur in the wrong direction.

As soon as the man left, Tina shoved her back into the container and said, "I can't believe he got me a stupid cat for my birthday. Not only do I hate cats, but I'm allergic to them."

Charcoal had no idea what that meant, but she knew that she did not like Tina.

Charcoal spent the next week locked in a dark closet. She was let out only when the man visited each evening. As soon as he'd leave, it was back in the closet again.

One evening after the man had left, Tina gave her an odd look and said, "I'm getting tired of this. I need to find some way to get rid of you without upsetting Todd. Maybe an accident, or better yet I'll drop you off somewhere and tell him you ran away."

A Charcoal Christmas

Two days later Tina drove Charcoal to a parking lot behind a vacant furniture store, released her and drove away. It was cold and snowing outside but she was just happy to be out of that closet and free.

Over the next three weeks, Charcoal learned that being free and on her own wasn't much fun. In her quest to reunite with her brothers and sisters, she encountered many obstacles. Mean dogs chased her up trees, cats fought her to protect their territory and cars tried to run her over.

Every day she had to hunt for food to survive, and each cold night she had to find a safe place to sleep where she'd be protected from the elements and her enemies. Most nights she'd close her eyes but never sleep. Every sound was a potential danger, so she always had to be ready to fight or run.

By the third week she was beginning to wonder if she'd ever find her way back to her kin. Then one day her nose picked up a familiar scent. It was the smell of Luigi's Pizzeria. Luigi's Pizzeria was located right next door to Johnson's Market, and Luigi the owner use to throw pizza scraps to her and her brothers and sisters. She was sure that she had found her way home, but the truth is it could have been any old pizzeria. As luck would have it, it really was Luigi's and she was indeed home again.

All excited, she ran behind the store and began looking for her family. Although she picked up the faint scent of her siblings, no one was around. Charcoal was so tired that she crawled under the safety of the loading dock and fell into a deep sleep.

For the next two days she looked everywhere for her family, but they were nowhere to be found.

Mr. Johnson spotted her one evening and said, "Is that you, Charcoal? What are you doing back here? I thought Animal Control took all of you away for good."

A Charcoal Christmas

She was so happy to see Mr. Johnson that she took a chance and rubbed her side against his leg. He reached down and stroked her softly down her back. Then he went inside and came back with food and water.

"Here you go, Charcoal. I'll let you hang around here as long as you stay out of my store. Do we have a deal? If I see you in the store I'm gonna have to call Animal Control."

Charcoal continued to rub against Mr. Johnson's leg.

"I'll take that as a yes," he said laughing. "I can't believe I'm talking to a cat."

As the days and weeks passed, Charcoal settled into her routine of hunting, eating and sleeping. After that misadventure with the man and Tina, she never ventured far from Johnson's Market and was leery of stranger's advances.

She began spending more and more of her day sitting at the front entrance of the store, watching people come and go. She enjoyed sitting there because when the automatic door opened she could feel the warmth from inside the store.

Most people were friendly and some would pet her and give her treats. Others were not so nice and would shoo her away, or bring their dogs and leave them tied up outside as they shopped. At first she'd run away when the dogs barked at her, but after a while she realized that the dogs couldn't harm her.

Charcoal kept hearing people mention the word Christmas. She had no idea what it meant, but she noticed that people who used it always acted friendly.

Her favorite days were Saturday and Wednesday, not that she knew them by those names, but she knew that on those days a boy named Joey came to the store with his mother. Joey had fallen in love with Charcoal the minute he saw her. Every visit he would run up to her, get down on his knees, give her a big hug and

A Charcoal Christmas

scratch behind her ears. At first she was a little frightened of Joey, but soon she realized that he wouldn't hurt her, and she began looking forward to his visits. She enjoyed the petting, hugs and all the attention he gave her.

Joey's mother wasn't as nice to her. She would always take Joey away and into the store.

Joey would say, "Mommy, she's so pretty and really friendly. Do you think that Daddy would let us take her home?"

"I don't think that's a good idea, honey. We don't know where that cat has been. Come on, let's get inside."

On the way out, Joey would always stop to hug her and say goodbye. There was something about him that made Charcoal happy every time she saw him.

This routine continued every Wednesday and Saturday, until one day Joey and his mother stopped coming. Two whole weeks went by before Joey and his mother reappeared. Charcoal was excited to see her friend, but Joey didn't stop this time. He walked right by without saying a word. Charcoal was confused and even tried meowing to get his attention, but Joey never looked at her or acknowledged her existence. She didn't know what was wrong but she knew that something had changed.

What Charcoal didn't know was that Joey's daddy had been killed in an automobile accident and that little Joey had gone into shock and stopped speaking. Joey's mother had tried everything to get him to speak, but he wouldn't. She was so worried about him that she took him to several doctors, but they all told her the same thing. There was nothing physically wrong with him; he was in shock over the sudden death of his father, and it would take time for him to process it. They told her to be patient and eventually he'd speak again.

Charcoal wished she could do something for her friend, but she had no idea what that could be. The last time they came to the store, Joey's mom stopped him in front of Charcoal and said, "Look honey, that little cat you love is calling you. Do you want to say hello?"

Joey said nothing and stared off into the distance. Joey's mother gave Charcoal a sad look, then took Joey by the hand and said, "Come on, baby, we need to go inside and order the Christmas turkey. Then we'll go shopping for your present. Would you like that?"

Again Joey said nothing.

Charcoal didn't know what to call it, but she knew she didn't like the way that Joey's sadness made her feel. She was 'heartbroken' that she'd lost her friend.

It was three days before Christmas and Charcoal took her place at the front entrance of the store. It was very quiet today and she noticed that people would come to the door but not go inside. She didn't understand what was wrong, but Mr. Johnson hadn't left her any food or water last night, and today the lights weren't on in the store. People would come to the front entrance, stare at something in the window and walk away.

If Charcoal could read, she would have known that Mr, Johnson had died of a heart attack yesterday afternoon. Sadly, her entire world was about to change, and she had no idea it was happening.

That night was a cold one. A mixture of snow and rain fell from the sky and there was still no Mr. Johnson or food in her bowl. It was too cold and wet to hunt for food, so she curled up under the loading dock, closed her eyes and went to sleep hungry.

It was two days before Christmas and fewer people showed up at the store entrance. Some kind souls came and brought her food, but it wasn't enough to fill her belly and certainly not enough to feed her tomorrow and the next day. She began to sense that something had happened to Mr. Johnson and

A Charcoal Christmas

she had no idea what she was going to do now. She knew she couldn't stay here anymore and was about to leave the front entrance, when she spotted Joey and his mother coming toward her.

Joey still didn't speak or look at her. His mother stared at something in the window and said, "Poor Mr. Johnson. He was such a nice man." Then she looked down at Charcoal, turned and began walking away.

Charcoal meowed several times, trying to get their attention, but they just kept walking. Without any food or a reason to stay, Charcoal decided she would follow them and see where they went. She had no idea where this would lead her, but it had to be better than freezing or starving under the loading dock.

She followed them up and down several neighborhood streets, keeping her distance so they wouldn't see her. They finally stopped in front of a little house surrounded by a white picket fence.

Joey's mother reached into the mailbox and said, "Look, Joey, you got Christmas cards from your cousins Paul and Ginger, and one from Auntie Jean. Let's go inside and open them."

Charcoal hid behind the fence until they were inside and watched as lights lit up in the window and on the Christmas tree. She was fascinated by the twinkling lights and decided to sneak closer to get a better look inside.

Joey was sitting in a chair holding the unopened Christmas cards in his hand. His face was sad and he stared up at the ceiling. His mother sat down beside him, opened one of the cards and read it out loud. Joey said nothing. He just sat there wiping his eyes.

"Would you like me to make some hot cocoa before we open the other cards?" his mother asked.

A Charcoal Christmas

Joey wiped his nose with his sleeve and continued to stare at the ceiling.

His mother took him by the hand and said, "Baby, I miss your daddy, too. He's looking down on us from heaven and he's very sad seeing you this way. He wants you to be happy, Joey. I promise you that someday you'll see him again."

When Joey didn't respond, his mother dropped her head in her hands and began to sob.

"Please come back to me, sweetheart. You're all I have in this world. Please don't leave me all alone, especially on this first Christmas without your daddy."

Charcoal watched as they both wept, and a deep guttural meow sound left her mouth. The wind was howling outside so Joey and his mother couldn't hear it, but Charcoal did it again and again. She felt a pain inside that she didn't understand and she didn't know how to make it feel better.

Charcoal watched as Joey hugged his mother and walked out of the room. She ran around to the side of the house and noticed a light in the window. It was getting really cold outside and she knew she had to find shelter for the night, but she couldn't pull herself away from Joey's house.

She jumped up on the window sill and watched as Joey pulled back the sheets and got into bed. Charcoal was having a difficult time standing on the narrow sill, and the snow and wind weren't making it any easier. Even though her fur had its thick winter coat she began to shiver as the wind penetrated her body. She wouldn't last long in this weather, but she couldn't bring herself to leave. The truth is, she had no place else to go.

She began to meow loudly, over and over again, but Joey didn't move. In a final effort to get his attention, she scratched at the window with her claws and smacked it hard with her tail.

A Charcoal Christmas

Joey sat up, stared at the window and watched as she continued to scratch and claw. She gave one last meow, and Joey got up out of bed and walked out of the room, instead of walking towards her.

Charcoal fell off the sill and laid down on the wet snow. Cold and shaking, she curled up into a ball and closed her eyes. If she laid here long enough she would never make it to celebrate her first birthday.

Suddenly she felt someone lift her off the ground and her body was floating in the air. She knew that someone had picked her up, but she was too cold and weak to fight. When she looked up she saw Joey's face. He had her in his arms and was opening the front door.

Joey's mother looked at him and said, "What were you doing outside without your winter coat and boots? Are you trying to make yourself sick?"

It took her several seconds before she realized what Joey was holding. It was the cat from Johnson's Market.

"Baby, you can't bring that animal inside the house," she said. "We have no idea where it's been or what it's come in contact with. What if it's sick or has rabies?"

Joey kept petting Charcoal and ignoring his mother's words.

"I'm sorry, Joey, but you'll have to put the cat back outside."

Joey looked up at her and spoke for the first time since the death of his father.

"If I leave her outside, Mommy, she'll die. I can't do that, Mommy," he replied, choked up with emotion.

A Charcoal Christmas

At the shock of hearing him speak, Joey's mother put a hand over her mouth and began to weep joyful tears.

"You spoke," she said as the tears trickled down her face.

"Please don't make me put her outside, Mommy. I don't want her to die like my Daddy. I couldn't save him but I can save her," he pleaded. "I promise that I'll always take care of her and love her for the rest of her life. Please don't make me put her outside. Please let me keep her. It's Christmas and it's the only present I want."

Under the circumstances, how could his mother say no?

"Okay Joey, you can keep her, but right after Christmas we'll have to take her for a checkup."

Little did Joey's mother know that Charcoal had already had her shots and was in very good health.

Joey looked at Charcoal and said, "Did you hear that girl? You can live with us."

He hugged her tight and listened as she began her happy purr.

"What will we name her?" asked his mother.

Joey thought about it and replied, "I think we should name her Georgia."

His daddy's name was George, and his mother realized that her son was paying tribute to his father by naming her Georgia.

Tears of joy once again ran down her cheeks as she said, "I think your Daddy would love that you gave her that name. How about we go in the kitchen and see if we can find something for little Georgia to eat?"

A Charcoal Christmas

That night, Georgia (also known as Charcoal) slept in a warm bed curled up beside her best friend.

After tucking them in, Joey's mother listened at the door as her son said his prayers.

"Daddy, if you can hear me, I want you to know that I miss you and I'm still sad inside, but I'm going to try to be happy on the outside. Thank you for telling Mommy to let me keep Georgia."

He reached over, kissed Georgia on the nose and said, "Merry Christmas, Daddy. I love you."

Christmas Mourning

Father Pedro glances around the church, then raises his arms as the parishioners stand for the final blessing.

"May the peace of the Lord be always with you," he says while making the sign of the cross. "Go in peace to serve the Lord. Merry Christmas, everyone."

"Merry Christmas, Father," the parishioners reply in unison.

It had snowed steadily for most of the day, and the temperature had fallen well below freezing. The snow was so deep that the snowplows were unable to keep the roadways clear, which explains why attendance at midnight mass on Christmas Eve was so sparse. A few brave souls had driven their cars, but most of the people in attendance were parishioners who lived within walking distance of the church.

Father Pedro stands in the foyer as the parishioners file out of the church. Many stop to shake his hand and exchange Christmas pleasantries, while others just wave and disappear into the white blanket of snow.

Father notices that Mrs. Bellino is once again in attendance without her husband. When their eighteen-year-old daughter Francesca died at the hands of a drunk driver, Mr. Bellino stopped attending mass. Mrs. Bellino asked Father Pedro to speak to her husband in an attempt to convince him to come back to the church, but as long as he continues to blame God for his daughter's tragic death, there's nothing that Father can say to make him return.

Father Pedro's attempt to comfort and explain the ways of the Lord fell on deaf ears. Mr. Bellino wanted Father to explain why God would take her in the prime of her life. What was the point of giving her life, if it could be taken so carelessly? Father Pedro had no answers. The truth is, he had no idea why God did what he did and often struggled to understand the randomness of life and death.

Ever since his younger brother Miguel had wasted away from the dreadful AIDS virus, he'd stopped trying to understand God's master plan.

Miguel was a kind and gentle soul who didn't deserve to die such a painful and tragic death. As a social worker, Miguel loved his work and honestly believed that he could make a difference in the lives of others. The man was a totally selfless human being who would give the shirt off his back, or money from his pocket, to anyone who truly needed it. Even though Miguel didn't believe in God or the ways of the Church, Father Pedro was still in awe of his brother and often referred to him as a saint.

Miguel had no interest in waiting for the afterlife or the Kingdom of Heaven; his focus was in making this world a better one, one person at a time. It was a severe blow to Father Pedro's faith when God took his brother away. Why the Lord had allowed his dear, sweet brother to be stricken with such an awful disease is something that to this day he'd been unable to reconcile. Why would such a vessel of kindness be removed from this world?

Ben Johnson shakes his hand firmly, drawing Father Pedro back into the moment.

"Merry Christmas, Father. That was a wonderful sermon tonight. My Sara would have loved it."

Christmas Mourning

"Thank you, Mr. Johnson. I'm sure Sara heard every word," Father Pedro replies, while placing a hand on the man's shoulder.

Mr. Johnson's wife had passed away giving birth to their first child. Unfortunately, the child (a boy) died one week later, leaving poor Ben's life in complete shambles. Why had God taken them away? What had he done to deserve such pain and sadness in his life? A Christian his entire life, Ben faithfully served his church and his community, treated everyone with kindness and compassion, and cherished his wife. All he wanted from Father Pedro was an explanation as to what he'd done to anger God in such a way that he would punish him by taking his family from him. In other words, he wanted answers to questions that Father couldn't provide.

All Father Pedro could do was recite the same, tired explanation about how God works in mysterious ways. How it's not for us to know or question why things happen, but to accept and know that God has a plan for each and every one of us. Father Pedro told him that his wife and child were in God's good graces in the Kingdom of Heaven, and someday Ben would see them again. Blah, blah, blah, even as he'd said it, Father Pedro realized how stale and hollow the explanation sounded.

After thirty years in the priesthood, he'd witnessed every form of human emotion life had to offer. He'd baptized, confirmed, married, and buried hundreds of people, but it was always the pain, sadness, and wickedness that stuck to him like tar paper. He always wondered why there wasn't enough good in the world to offset all of the evil that people do. Perhaps there was enough love and kindness on this planet, but in his profession he'd experienced more pain and sorrow than love and happiness.

After so many years of dealing with death and mourning, he'd come to dread funerals and hospital visits. It was so bad that he felt physically ill before performing a funeral mass or visiting the sick. He pleaded with God every day to give him the strength to comfort the sick and suffering, and the courage to carry on with

Christmas Mourning

his service to the church and community. He prayed long and hard for the souls of the dead and the living, but in the end, Father Pedro wasn't sure if praying made any difference in their lives or deaths.

When he graduated from the seminary as a young and ambitious priest, it was easy to believe that he could make a difference in people's lives. Without any real world experience, it's easy to believe that your strength and faith can propel you to achieve the lofty goals you set for yourself. Only after years of religious service does reality smack you in the face and force you to confront the tragedy that is inherent in everyday life. For some, life is beautiful, their wants and needs are easily satisfied, but for most, life is cold, brutal, and unforgiving. After thirty years of fighting the good fight, Father Pedro had come to the sad conclusion that there isn't a damn thing he can say or do to stop the parade of pain and suffering.

What do you say to grieving parents whose child is born with leukemia? Trust in God and everything will be okay? What about the fiancée whose future husband is murdered a week before the wedding? Trust in God... he has a plan? How about parents who are killed in an automobile accident, leaving their young children behind? Don't worry, Mommy and Daddy are in heaven? How does any of that make any sense? We are always left with the question: Why?

Father Pedro, so deep within his thoughts, doesn't notice that the last parishioner had left the church. He listens to the echo of his footsteps as he walks through the church to the sacristy.

As he's removing his stole and garments, the music director and altar servers stop by to wish him a merry Christmas.

"See you tomorrow morning at eleven o'clock mass," says David, the church music director.

"Sleep well and merry Christmas to you and your family, David."

"You too, Father. Good night."

After everyone has left, Father Pedro walks out into the dark church and kneels before the altar.

"Lord, if you're listening, please forgive me for what I'm about to do."

He stands, makes the sign of the cross, and walks out of the church, locking the door behind him.

The wind howls and swirls powdery snow into his face as he struggles to make his way across the empty parking lot towards the rectory. The ground is icy, but he manages to stay on his feet until he reaches the front door. His hands are frozen as he struggles to insert the key into the lock. Finally succeeding, the door swings open and a blast of warmth hits him.

It's a blessed Christmas morning, but the rectory feels like a dark, silent tomb. Father Francis Delaney, the head pastor and Father Pedro's mentor, has only been dead two months, but his death has left a giant void in Father Pedro's life. Whenever Father Pedro felt depressed and insecure about his faith, Father Francis had always been there to pick him up and impart the words of wisdom he'd needed to carry on. Now without his friend, the darkness is slowly creeping back into his soul, and he doesn't know how to make it stop.

He can still recall what Father Francis had told him while he administered the last rites to his friend and mentor. Father Francis took his hand and whispered, "It will be okay, Pedro. You have to be strong and believe that in the end, what you do is of great value and that some day we will see each other again."

"I don't know what I'll do without you, Francis. I don't know if I can keep the darkness from destroying me. I want to believe so badly, but a part of me needs proof. A part of me wants to know that there's more to life then this sad world we live in."

Christmas Mourning

"Would it give you hope and comfort, if I promise to send you a sign?"

"A sign?"

"Yes. I'll send you a sign that death is not final. A sign proving that our souls carry on beyond this mortal world of flesh and bones."

"Others before you have tried without success, Francis. What makes you think that your attempt will be different?"

Father Francis coughed and said, "Have I ever let you down, my dear Pedro? God willing, I'll do everything in my power to send you a sign. You're too good a man and priest to fall into a pit of despair. The people need you."

For two months Father Pedro had waited patiently for Father Francis's sign, but nothing happened. No visitation in the night, no epiphany behind the altar, no miracles for the sick or dying, and no whispers from God in his ear.

Father Francis's sixteen-year-old collie, Biscuit, lay sleeping in the corner. Father Pedro cleans and tops off her food and water bowl, then heads down to the basement, locking the door behind him.

The rectory basement contains the church library, the office, and a safe, where all the mass collections are temporarily stored. The furniture is old yet functional, and the room is the perfect place for priests to speak privately and unwind after a long day. He and Father Francis had spent many enjoyable hours in this room discussing life, faith, and their insecurities. The memories of his longtime friend filled every inch of the room.

Father Pedro unlocks the safe and removes a sealed envelope, a bottle of Jim Beam whiskey, and a small metal box. He takes one of the Vatican souvenir shot glasses he'd brought back from his 2008 trip to Rome and fills it with whiskey. He downs one shot and quickly refills the glass while staring at the words he'd written on the envelope containing his final goodbye.

To Whom It May Concern

That about sums it up, he thinks, as he drinks the second shot of whiskey and sits back, feeling the warm liquor burning his throat. He places the metal box on his lap and fiddles with the combination lock until it pops open. He stares at the object in the box and then pours himself another drink, trying to work up the courage to do what needs to be done.

His throat is now coated with whiskey, and this third shot feels smooth and satisfying as it slips down his throat. The alcohol is doing its job, a few more hits and he believes he'll be ready. Sadly, he realizes that this is the first time in a long time that he's unafraid and in control of his fragile emotions.

He hears the wind rattle against the basement windows, pelting them with a mixture of snow and ice. He raises his glass one more time, then pulls the gun from the metal box and places it on his lap. The bottle of Jim Beam is half empty, and he's feeling pretty good as he releases the safety catch. He takes one last drink as he checks to make sure the gun is loaded. He closes his eyes, raises the gun to the side of his temple, and begins to weep softly.

He whispers, "Lord, give me one good reason why I shouldn't do this. I'm tired of living a life of sadness, misery, and pain. Please, give me one stinking sign. Just one little sign to show me that you care and that my life is worth living."

The room is silent.

Suddenly Father Pedro jumps at the unexpected sound coming from one of the basement windows. In that moment, he realizes that had his finger been on the trigger, he'd probably be dead right now. Instead he stands up, staring at a long-haired black cat who is clawing at the window and meowing loudly. The poor cat is covered in snow and ice and continues to meow and claw at the window.

"For goodness sake, go away."

The cat stares at him, its large black eyes begging him to open the window.

"I don't believe this," he says as he walks to the window and pounds on the glass, attempting to frighten the cat away.

"Go away. You don't want to be in here with me."

The cat ignores his pounding and continues staring at Father Pedro. Perhaps it's just an illusion or too much whiskey, but it appears to Father that tears are falling from its eyes.

He places the gun down and unlatches the window, allowing the cat to jump down into the warm basement.

"Suit yourself, Cat," he says, slurring his words. "Your being here isn't going to change what's about to happen."

He grabs the gun, sits in the chair, places the barrel against his temple, and closes his eyes. As he attempts to work up the nerve to pull the trigger, he feels something cold and wet jump on his lap. He looks down and sees the cat sitting on him. The poor thing is so cold that it shivers violently, trying to find warmth as it cuddles against him. Overtaken with compassion for this helpless creature, he places the gun down and wraps his arms around the cat.

They sit quietly for several minutes as Father Pedro strokes the cat, reassuring it that everything will be fine. The cat rubs its wet fur against his face and purrs gently. Before they know it, the warm and relaxing moment they share leads to a deep and peaceful sleep.

Father Pedro dreams that he's a child again, rocking gently in his mother's arms. She's singing him a lullaby as his eyes struggle to remain open. When his eyes finally shut, he feels safe, secure, and loved.

Several hours later, his peaceful bliss is interrupted by a loud knocking sound and a muffled voice frantically calling his name.

"Father Pedro, is everything okay? Are you asleep in there? Please answer me, or I'll call the police."

Reluctantly, he opens his eyes and notices the morning sun pour through the icy windows. The clock on the mantel reads quarter after ten.

"I'll be right out, Mrs. Leary."

"Sorry to bother you, Father, but I had to wake you, or you'll be late for morning mass."

"I'll be upstairs in a moment," he says while staring at the gun, envelope, and nearly empty bottle of whiskey.

The cat is still curled in his lap, awake and looking up at him.

"What are you looking at?" he says and smiles. "I guess you saved my life last night, but I'm not sure whether to thank you or wring your neck."

The cat stands up, sniffs Father's breath, and gives him a nasty look. Father Pedro bursts out in laughter and strokes the cat's head.

He lifts the cat up and places his nose against the cat's and says, "I guess I better clean up down here before going upstairs. Merry Christmas, Mr. Cat. Thank you for saving my life."

As he holds the cat, he notices that beneath the thick fur there's a collar with an identification tag.

His eyes fill with tears as he reads the inscription. He clutches the cat and squeezes it tightly against his body. The inscription reads.

This cat belongs to Mary. Reward offered if found. Please call.

Below the telephone number he notices the cat's name printed in large bold letters.

FRANCIS.

A Message from the Author

I hope you enjoyed reading this book as much as I enjoyed writing it.

As a self-published independent author I don't have the financial resources to advertise my books to a mass audience, so I rely on wonderful readers like you to help spread the word. If you enjoyed what you read, I hope you'll tell your friends and family about it.

Reviews are essential to any book's success. If you can spare a moment to leave a short review on Amazon or Goodreads it would be gratefully appreciated.

Peace.

About the Author

John D. Ottini resides in Orlando, Florida with his wife and best friend Nancy and a mischievous black and white tabby named Bella.

Visit My Blog

jdonovels.wordpress.com

amazon.com/author/johnottini

Books by John D. Ottini

People Behaving Badly: A Collection of Short Mystery Stories

A Reason to Kill: Collected Mystery Stories

(Available at Amazon.com or Createspace.com)

Made in the USA
Monee, IL
19 December 2020